DUST

The story of the Original Tooth Fairy

Written By: Audrey Willett & Paulette Harper
Illustrated By: Dave O' Connell

THE STORY OF THE ORIGINAL TOOTH FAIRY

iUniverse books may be ordered through booksellers or by contacting:

iUniverse
1663 Liberty Drive
Bloomington, IN 47403
www.iuniverse.com
844-349-9409

ISBN: 978-1-6632-6778-8 (sc)
ISBN: 978-1-6632-6779-5 (hc)
ISBN: 978-1-6632-6780-1 (e)

Library of Congress Control Number: 2024921491

Print information available on the last page.

iUniverse rev. date: 11/27/2024

For Jared, Avrey, Sailor and Finley -

We dedicate this story to the magic of imagination,
the wonder of childhood, and the joy of believing
in what can't always be seen. May you always
hold close the traditions that make you smile and
remember that anything is possible if you believe.

With all our love,

Audrey Willett & Paulette Harper

And to our moms Pauline and Joleen -
who never stopped believing.

Allow me to introduce
myself.
I am the Original
Tooth Fairy.

My name is DUST. It
is very nice to finally
meet you.

1

What I am about to tell you has been kept a secret for a very long time. Can you keep a secret? I want to tell you my story...

I come from a small village deep in the woods where fairies and elves live. There are many small villages like this all over the world. We like to live where there is little human activity, but let's keep this just between us.

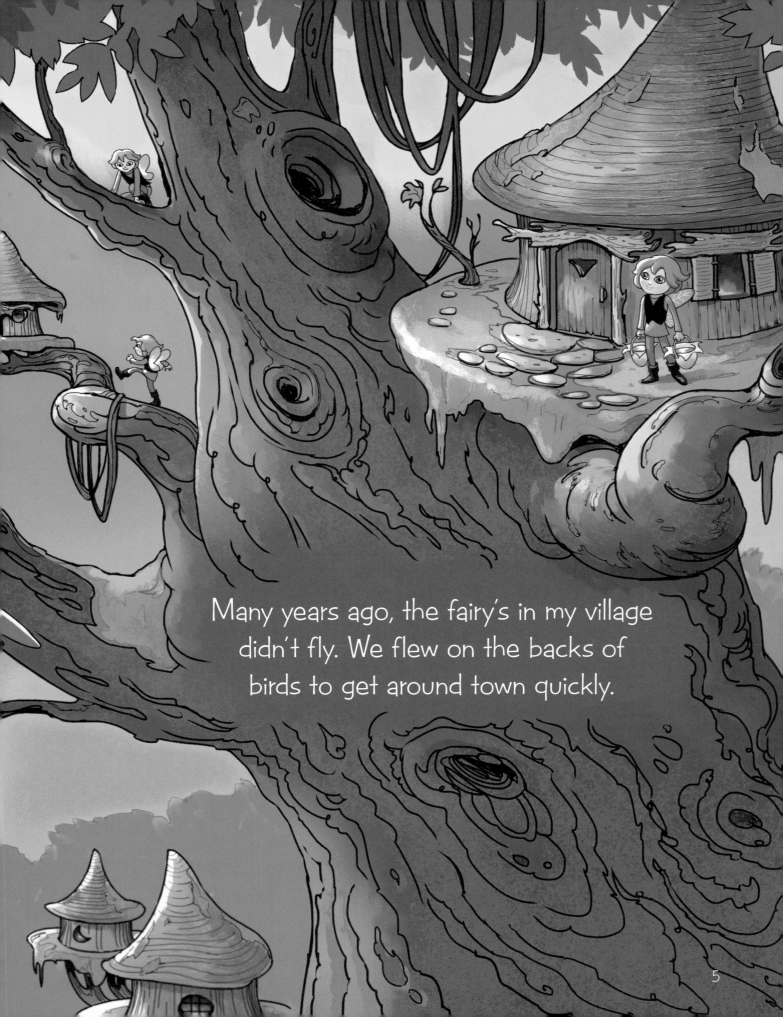

Many years ago, the fairy's in my village
didn't fly. We flew on the backs of
birds to get around town quickly.

It wasn't until one day I saw my friend Perez, a mouse, hiding what I thought was a diamond. I was curious and asked him what he was doing.

Perez told me he was hiding a baby tooth that he got from a little girl. He said baby teeth are very special and very hard to find.

On my birthday February 29th, Perez gave me a baby tooth. This is the day that changed my life forever.

Now pay close attention to what I am about to tell you next. I wasn't sure what to do with the baby tooth. Perez said it was very special, but he did not tell me how or why it was so special.

I banged it - nothing happened.

I put it under a light – nothing

I put it in water - still nothing.

I decided to grind the baby tooth on a hard brick to see what it was made of. I was making a bit of a mess when something incredible started to happen.

As I ground down the baby tooth,
I began to feel an incredible
sensation, my wings began to flutter.
It was then, at that moment, that
I knew this was more than just a
baby tooth. It was magic dust.

And I loved it!!

I was now a
flying fairy.

It took me a few tries before I finally got the hang of flying. The only problem is after a few days my wings stopped fluttering and the magic from the dust fades away.

When my dust was about to run out, my wings would feel heavy, they couldn't lift me anymore. I realized the magic doesn't last forever and I had to find more dust.

There was a town close by where children were playing. I could hear them laughing.

There was a little girl who was wiggling her front tooth. "What luck", I thought. She may lose her tooth today.

I followed the little girl home and watched her through the window.

The little girl was brushing her teeth before going to bed. I was just about to give up and fly home when she started to wiggle her loose tooth. "Oh, yeah baby!" I said. It came out. She looked at it curiously and inspected it. Then she walked to her bed, made a wish, placed it under her pillow and went to sleep.

I snuck into her bedroom after she fell asleep.
I had to be so quiet as to not get caught.

It took all of my strength and skill to
get that baby tooth out from under
her pillow without waking her up.

Once I got the tooth, I thought I should
leave her something in return. I had some
money in my pocket, I placed it under
her pillow where the tooth had been.

I waited all night until the next morning when she woke
up to make sure she was not upset with the exchange.
When she woke up she checked under her pillow and she
seemed very happy. She yelled for her mom and dad to
come and see. They seemed surprised and excited as well.

I can keep coming back to collect her baby teeth. I researched and found out children lose up to 20 baby teeth. That's a lot of DUST!!

This is when the term "Tooth Fairy" began.
Soon all of the fairies in town wanted to fly just like me.
In time each fairy had a child of their own to look after.

Like many people you know, we all have jobs to earn money around town. I use to be a delivery fairy. Now I am the Original Tooth Fairy and it is a full time career. Although I have many associates, they still look to me for guidance and direction. It's a very important job that I love and take seriously.

After over 100 years of collecting baby teeth, I have learned there are many different types of DUST depending on the quality of the tooth. The cleaner your baby teeth, the stronger the fairy dust and longer it lasts for us. It is very important to brush your teeth and keep them clean. I love candy and sweets like everyone else, but teeth with cavities equals bad dust.

Let me explain how this works. The day you lose your tooth, your personal fairy is assigned to you. Your fairy has been secretly watching you and waiting for you tooth. Place you tooth under your pillow. Once you are asleep, your fairy will take your tooth and leave a gift in exchange. The gift I leave depends on how clean the tooth is and the mood I am in that day.

Don't worry if your tooth falls out
and you can't find it. I just found
one in the grass that a boy named
Jared lost while playing ball.

The tooth fairy always knows where your teeth are. Just leave a note under your pillow if you lost your tooth and you will still get a gift in return.

One last thing, if by chance you notice in the morning your tooth is still there, don't be alarmed, that just means you were not in a deep enough sleep. The tooth fairy will keep coming back until it is safe to make the exchange and not get caught.

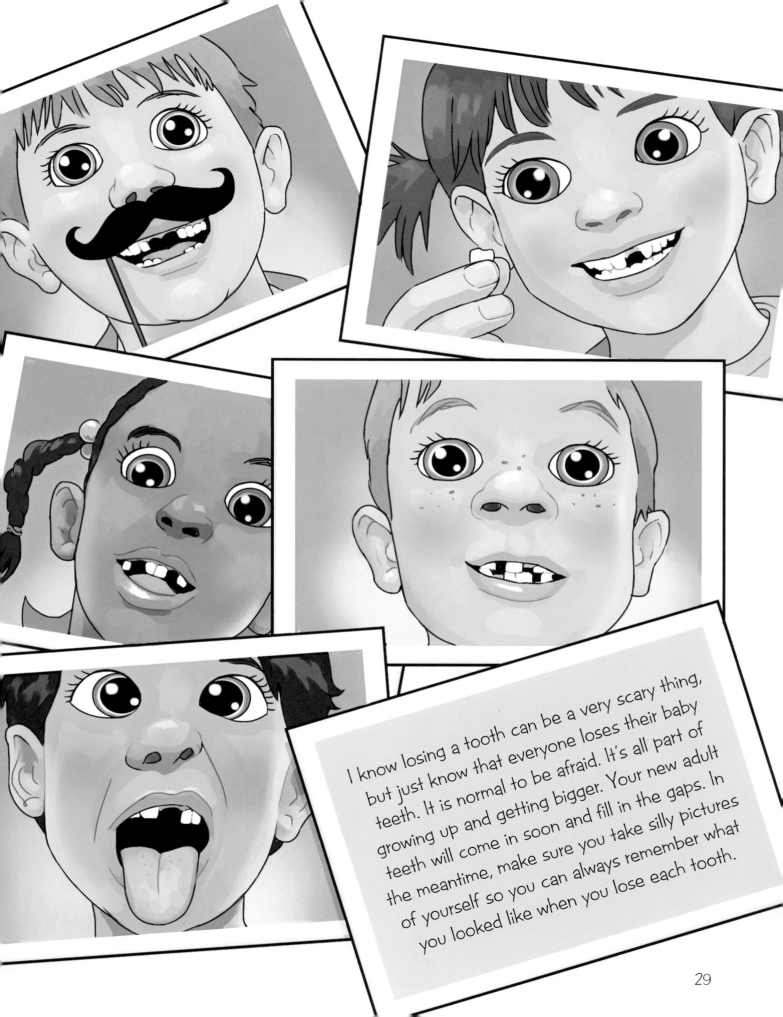

I know losing a tooth can be a very scary thing, but just know that everyone loses their baby teeth. It is normal to be afraid. It's all part of growing up and getting bigger. Your new adult teeth will come in soon and fill in the gaps. In the meantime, make sure you take silly pictures of yourself so you can always remember what you looked like when you lose each tooth.

29

Do me a favor and keep brushing and flossing so your teeth are clean and bright. Remember the cleaner the tooth, the better the dust to keep us flying high and fast. Bye for now.

Sincerely,

DUST,
The Original
Tooth Fairy

Printed in the United States
by Baker & Taylor Publisher Services